Netherlands

by Thomas Persano

Consultant: Marjorie Faulstich Orellana, PhD
Professor of Urban Schooling
University of California, Los Angeles

BEARPORT
PUBLISHING

New York, New York

Credits

Cover, © LSOphoto/iStock and © Olena Z/Shutterstock; TOC, © Vndrpttn/iStock; 4, © AleksandarGeorgiev/iStock; 5L, © Westend61 GmbH/Alamy; 5B, © adisa/iStock; 7, © Ger Beekes/Alamy; 8–9, © photonaj/iStock; 9R, © JacobH/iStock; 10L, © Jmrocek/iStock; 10R, © Mirko Graul/Shutterstock; 11T, © taviphoto/iStock; 11B, © Petr Simon/iStock; 12, © Rijksmuseum/Bridgeman Images; 13, © Ben Schonewille/Shutterstock; 14, © bpperry/iStock; 15T, © S. Borisov/Shutterstock; 15B, © BrasilNut1/iStock; 16, © kavalenkau/Shutterstock; 17, © Bumble Dee/Shutterstock; 18L, © karandaev/iStock; 18–19, © JacobH/iStock; 19R, © Lena_Zajchikova/iStock; 20, © studioportosabbia/iStock; 21T, © ALLEKO/iStock; 21B, © ranasu/iStock; 22, © RockerStocker/Shutterstock; 23, © Lev Dolgachov/Alamy; 24, © Monkey Business Images/Shutterstock; 25T, © Kerem Gogus/Dreamstime; 25B, © Aijaistock/iStock; 26, © Rana Royalty free/Alamy; 27T, © Ian Dagnall/Alamy; 27B, © Dennis van de Water/Shutterstock; 28T, © Nancy Beijersbergen/Shutterstock; 28B, © Apion/Shutterstock; 29, © FamVeld/Shutterstock; 30T, © Viktor Kunz/Shutterstock and © spinetta/Shutterstock; 30B, © RossHelen/Shutterstock; 31 (T to B), © OlgaPonomarenko/Shutterstock, © Adisa/Shutterstock, © S-F/Shutterstock, © Roel Slootweg/Shutterstock, © Valerii Honcharuk/Dreamstime, and © Gertjan Hooijer/Shutterstock; 32, © Mitrofanov Alexander/Shutterstock.

Publisher: Kenn Goin
Senior Editor: Joyce Tavolacci
Creative Director: Spencer Brinker
Design: Debrah Kaiser
Photo Researcher: Thomas Persano

Library of Congress Cataloging-in-Publication Data

Names: Persano, Thomas, author.
Title: Netherlands / by Thomas Persano.
Description: New York, New York: Bearport Publishing, [2020] | Series:
   Countries we come from | Includes bibliographical references and index.
Identifiers: LCCN 2019015055 (print) | LCCN 2019015539 (ebook) | ISBN
   9781642805871 (ebook) | ISBN 9781642805338 (library)
Subjects: LCSH: Netherlands—Juvenile literature.
Classification: LCC DJ18 (ebook) | LCC DJ18 .P43 2020 (print) | DDC
   949.2—dc23
LC record available at https://lccn.loc.gov/2019015055

For more information, write to Bearport Publishing Company, Inc., 45 West 21st Street, Suite 3B, New York, New York 10010. Printed in the United States of America.

10 9 8 7 6 5 4 3 2 1

Contents

This Is the Netherlands

BEAUTIFUL

Lively

MAJESTIC

5

The Netherlands is a small country in Europe.

It borders the North Sea.

Over 17 million people live there.

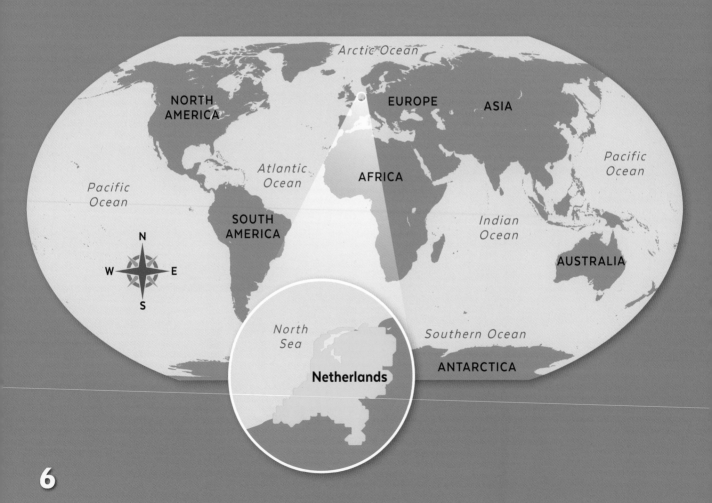

The people of the Netherlands call themselves *Nederlanders* (NEE-dur-lan-durz). They're also known as the *Dutch*.

The Netherlands is a very flat country.
Half of the land was once covered
by seawater.

Long ago, the Dutch built **dikes** around the flooded land.

Then, they pumped out the water.

The Dutch used windmills to help drain water from the land. Windmills are machines that run on wind power.

windmill

What animals live in the Netherlands?
You can spot hedgehogs and hares.

hedgehog

hare

There are **reptiles**, too.

Sand lizards scurry over dunes near the sea.

sand lizard

The Netherlands is home to many birds. One of the most striking is the black woodpecker.

11

The Netherlands has a long history.

Spain controlled the land for centuries.

The Dutch fought Spain for power during the Eighty Years' War (1568–1648).

Dutch and Spanish war ships

Later, France ruled the Netherlands.

The Netherlands is often called Holland.

In 1815, the Netherlands became fully **independent**.

Amsterdam is the **capital** of the Netherlands.

It's also the country's biggest city.

It's known for its many **canals** and bridges.

a canal in Amsterdam

There are over 1,200 bridges in Amsterdam!

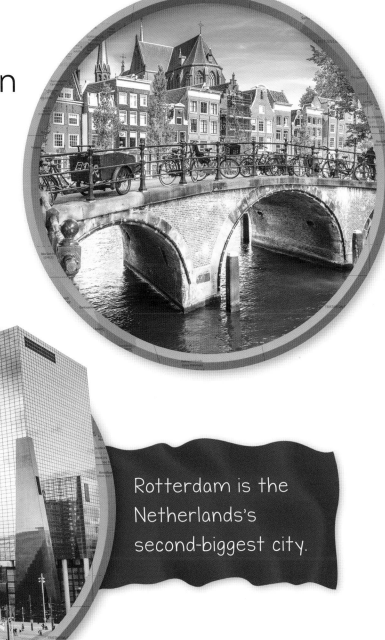

Rotterdam is the Netherlands's second-biggest city.

How do Dutch people get around?
They often ride bikes.

There are three times more bikes
than cars in the country!

A popular type of Dutch bike has a big bucket on the front. Children sometimes ride in it!

Bakfiets.nl

The Netherlands is famous for flowers.

Huge fields of tulips cover the country.

Each year, the Dutch produce billions of tulip and other flower **bulbs**.

They're shipped all over the world.

tulips

In the 1600s, tulip bulbs were used as money!

Dutch food is delicious!

Bitterballen (bih-TUR-ball-uhn) is a popular snack.

It's a fried meatball.

In winter, people enjoy *stamppot* (stam-POT).

This dish is made from potatoes, vegetables, and sausage.

A favorite treat is a *stroopwafel* (STROP-vaf-uhl). It's a caramel waffle cookie.

The main language of the Netherlands is Dutch.

This is how you say *thank you* in Dutch:

Dank je (DANK yah)

This is how you say *goodbye*:

Tot ziens (TOHT zeens)

Over 90 percent of Dutch people speak English!

The Dutch love soccer.

It's their favorite sport.

Korfball is another popular sport.

This game is similar to basketball.

Dutch sports teams and fans wear orange. Why? It's the national color of the Netherlands.

Some of the world's greatest artists are Dutch.

They include Rembrandt and Van Gogh.

Rembrandt is best known for his portraits.

a self-portrait by Rembrandt

Van Gogh often painted colorful flowers!

Van Gogh's sunflowers

The Rijksmuseum (RIKES-myoo-SEE-uhm) is a big museum in Amsterdam. It holds over one million pieces of art!

Around 17 million people visit the Netherlands each year.

They enjoy seeing the windmills in summer.

Wooden shoes called clogs are popular in the Netherlands. Many visitors buy them as a keepsake.

In winter, people love skating on the frozen canals!

Fast Facts

Capital city: Amsterdam

Population of the Netherlands: Over 17 million

Main language: Dutch

Money: Euro

Major religions: Catholic, Protestant, and Muslim

Neighboring countries: Belgium and Germany

Cool Fact: Raw onion and herring, a type of fish, is a popular Dutch snack!

bulbs (BUHLBZ) underground plant parts from which some plants grow

canals (kuh-NALZ) human-made waterways used by boats

capital (KAP-uh-tuhl) the city where a country's government is based

dikes (DIKES) high walls built to hold back water

independent (in-duh-PEN-dunt) free from outside control

reptiles (REP-tilez) cold-blooded animals, such as lizards, snakes, and crocodiles

Index

Read More

Murray, Julie. *Netherlands (Explore the Countries).* Minneapolis, MN: Big Buddy Books (2017).

Owings, Lisa. *The Netherlands (Exploring Countries).* Minneapolis, MN: Bellwether (2013).

Learn More Online

To learn more about the Netherlands, visit
www.bearportpublishing.com/CountriesWeComeFrom

About the Author

Thomas Persano lives in New York City.
He loves to travel and hopes to skate
along the frozen canals of Amsterdam
with his wife, Molly, one day.